BUG

Hannah Rappaport

Owl King Publishing, LLC   Orange, CT

Bug

Library of Congress Control Number: 2011934604

First Owl King Publishing Edition: August 2011

Printed in the United States of America

This book is dedicated to ...

My parents, you've helped me SO much to do this and feel good about myself, and you always bring that ant on the floor outside when you really don't want to

My friends and family, you're always right by my side

My teachers, you put in so much time to help me grow

Twiddle, may you rest in peace

And anyone who cares about bugs just as much as I do

So if your reflex when you see a bug is to squish, slap, or stomp, this dedication page isn't for you at all!

BUG

Contents

CHAPTER 1

Cali walked off the bus to excited laughter. Everyone was happy that she wasn't there. Nobody cared for Cali's petite, awkward shyness, especially the other children at her school. To Cali, they were all bullies, constantly teasing her for her raggedy, light brown hair and messy clothes. Cali knew that the outside didn't matter, so she really didn't care. She also knew that bullies just wanted to put others down so they could seem greater. She never stood up to them, though. She always just ignored them, because she didn't want trouble. Her father, who was serving in the army, told her not to brew up trouble — her dear, lovable, laughing father, who she never once took her mind off of in the course of an average day.

The stone path to Cali's front door was winding, for the Stills were quiet people. Well, at least Cali and her mom were. Cali's little brother, Caius, was born a month after Cali's father left, when Cali was five. Before then, Cali had still been quiet, but a faint smile was always on her face. When her father left, that smile instantly faded into a pursed, straight line. At age 11, the smile still hadn't returned.

Her mother's face had been tired and anxious after her husband left, until her baby boy was born, of course. She looked down at him, and he softly gurgled. She named him Caius, rejoice in Latin, because he had made her life a bit brighter. Now, at age 6, he was still her love and joy, but Cali's pain in the neck. Her mother often left her all alone to do whatever on her laptop so she could play with Caius, a plump, spoiled little boy that never paid any attention to Cali, either. His high, screechy giggling made him nothing like Cali or her mom.

As Cali reached her house, she sighed at the peeled paint, the air from her mouth visible in the cold winter air. The family could just barely pay for their house and food with a single mom making money from home and taking care of two kids. Cali sometimes wondered what it would be like to live in a mansion rather than a ranch house itching for repair, but, to not give her mom more to think about, she kept her thoughts to herself.

She let herself in the house, threw off her heavy exoskeleton of winter attire, and walked past her mom and Caius, who were playing with blocks in the family room. Caius came home from school earlier than Cali, and she hated that. It wasn't that learning wasn't appealing, because it was — Cali looked forward to being smarter every day with the new things she could discover in school. It was actually because nobody paid attention to her, except, of course, to make that mean comment about her outfit. She really wished that she could be in kindergarten, when things were less complicated and much mellower. At the beginning of kindergarten, she had her dad full time, too, instead of just on holidays.

Cali walked slowly to her small room; her backpack lazily rested on her arm. She laid her backpack on the handle of the door and gazed around the one place that was all hers. Her bed was just big enough for her to sleep in and her dresser and desk just large enough to fit clothes in and work at. Her father, serving in the army, told her not to ever have more than you need. That wonderfully kind man her brain was set to think about. On the back wall was a mural of a small, grassy field with three cows in it. One large bull, one medium cow, and one just a mere calf, just the way Cali wanted her life to be.

She sat on her bed across from the wall and stared at it. It seemed like the little calf's eye was moving!

"Ahhhhh!" she screamed, the rest of the family not even noticing.

Cali trembled as she walked closer, analyzing the moving eye, which turned out to not be an eye at all.

It was really a small, brown beetle, slowly moving its way across her room on the wall.

"Bug," whispered Cali, and let it crawl onto her finger. Her faint smile returned to her face for just an instant.

CHAPTER 2

Cali was a vegetarian ever since she knew how to think for herself. She always loved the quiet ways of animals, and she sometimes compared herself to one of them. She couldn't ever imagine eating one of her brethren.

She had always longed for a pet, something that would actually pay attention to her, but, as a young child, her parents didn't think she was ready for one. When she was older, her father left for the army, and there was already too much to take care of. Cali made dinner when she could and always kept her room spotless, because there wasn't much else to do but clean without any friends to go somewhere with.

Strangely, Cali always had a connection to bugs. While the other kids in kindergarten were squishing ants, Cali was watching in awe them carry bits and pieces of different foods to their home. She even let them crawl on her finger to get a tickly sensation that only little creatures running across your hand can give you. It really was magical.

One day in first grade, Cali had been fondly watching a caterpillar munch on a maple leaf, when Eliza walked over to her.

Eliza was the teacher's pet, always answering questions and looking cute while doing it. All the teachers adored her for her kindness to other students and politeness to everyone, except Cali of course. Nobody actually cared for Cali, especially not Eliza. At every recess, Eliza made up a new insult for Cali, each one more offending than the other.

Eliza flicked the caterpillar from the leaf onto the asphalt, and sneered as she took big steps (at least for a first grader), to its new spot, getting ready to step on it.

"No!" screamed Cali, breaking out of her quietness. She couldn't let the innocent caterpillar be killed!

Cali ran over to Eliza, pushed her away, and placed the caterpillar on the grass, not knowing what she had done.

"Teacher!" yelled Eliza in her screechy, annoying voice. "Cali pushed me!"

Yes, Cali had pushed her, but the tattletale Eliza hadn't been hurt at all, especially not compared to the pain of the caterpillar if she hadn't been pushed.

A recess monitor immediately ran over, hugging Eliza while looking at Cali with eyebrows almost down to her nose.

"Cali, you know we don't touch our friends, especially not to hurt them! What were you thinking?!" she demanded.

Tears rolled down Cali's cheeks and onto her ragged jumper.

"I, I didn't mean to push Eliza," she whispered. "I was just ..."

"Tell me as we go to the principal's office," the teacher broke in.

As they walked away, Eliza grinned evilly at Cali who was longingly looking towards the caterpillar now crawling safely up a tree. She disobeyed the teacher to defend herself on the walk to the principal's office, because she knew she was already in trouble. Her dad, who had just left for the army, had told her not to get into trouble and she had disobeyed him, which was much worse. Cali looked at her feet the rest of the way through the building, not wanting to have anything to do with bugs ever again.

As the beetle walked on Cali's finger, she felt very guilty. Her dad didn't like her touching bugs since he heard about her bug incident in first grade. He would be coming home for his birthday, February 10th.

Cali decided to let the bug outside to live. She opened the front door with the bug still on her finger and got ready to put it on the grass — make that snow. It was snowing and freezing outside, since it was January. Cali couldn't let the bug out now!

"Cali, why's the door open? You'll let in the cold air!" Mrs. Still yelled from the other room, tiredly.

"Um, I wanted to, er, um ..." Cali didn't quite know what to say, and she surely didn't want to lie to her mom, breaking her dad's rule.

"Whatever, luv, just close it when you're done," Cali's mom replied, sounding more tired than ever.

Cali immediately shut the door and ran to her room, closing that door as well.

She looked at the bug, its six legs idle and its small eyes staring. She couldn't do anything with it but keep it, so she did.

Cali got a shoebox and placed a wet sponge in the box, along with a pencil for it to climb on, which was enough for now. Then she put the bug inside and covered the top of the box with plastic wrap that she snuck from the kitchen so she could see in. She poked three small holes in the wrap with a pencil so it could breathe.

Content, Cali went onto her laptop to find out what she had just discovered in her room.

She typed in "brown, ¾ inch — long beetle of Connecticut" in the search engine bar. What came up was information on many different bugs and beetles, but only one looked just like hers: a western conifer seed bug, eating pinecone seeds of conifers, giving off an odor if threatened, and being a nuisance in homes in winter.

"Wow," thought Cali, not mad at herself for taking some strange insect under her wing, but excited that she was taking on the challenge of providing for an amazing creature.

Cali looked happily through the plastic wrap at the bug.

CHAPTER 3

Cali's mother never noticed the bug in Cali's room. She was much too busy getting herself ready for work and preparing Caius for school. It was perfect at this moment in time for her not to pay attention to Cali.

Her mom had never been fond of bugs. In preschool, when Cali used to bring them into the house, Mrs. Still had a screaming fit. She ran and hopped onto a kitchen chair at the sight of an ant on the floor. And spiders — that was another story.

Cali's dad tolerated bugs as long as they weren't in the house until the incident in first grade, but that was acceptable.

Basically, if Cali were caught with a bug in the house, she'd be punished big time.

Cali got to her lonely seat on the back of the bus. She stared longingly out the window at the fresh white snow. Winter, she believed, was the most magical time of the year. Everything was so crisp and clean, and no problems ever lasted long. They were cleaned, too. The first day of snow was the best, but then cars tracked mud on it, and nothing seemed so magical anymore. Today it was gorgeous though, and everybody was quiet on the bus, longing to frolic in the winter air. The school had believed 3 inches wasn't enough to cancel classes, to everyone's disappointment.

Cali, though, was not only thinking about the new snow but also about her little bug at home.

"Was it hungry?" she pondered in math, stumbling upon the fractions that looked almost like the beetle.

"If it is, will it starve?" she wondered in science, almost shocking herself when making a circuit.

"If it doesn't starve, how will I find pinecone seeds to prevent it from starving?" she asked herself in art, to find that she had made no progress on her paper Mache.

Finally, the art teacher, Mr. Mally, noticed the lack of growth in Cali's sculpture and casually strolled over.

"You haven't made much progress, Cal, and you're my star student! What's up?" he asked, patiently shadowing Cali's shoulder.

"Nothing, Mr. Mally. Really ... I'll get back to work. Sorry," she shamefully responded.

Mr. Mally shrugged, and walked slowly back to his desk, examining the other kids' work.

"Cali's daydreaming!" smirked Juanita, in her awful taunting laugh. "Is she in loooove? Or is she thinking about something dumb like she does all day?"

Cali forgot about Bug, if that's what she would call it.

"No!" she muttered. "Please stop."

"Hahaha!" guffawed Linda. "She's denying it!"

Cali painfully stared down at the paper mache and worked very quickly, in order to block out her surroundings.

"Yeah, get back to work, Cali. Work fast ... and no daydreaming!" Juanita laughed, almost falling over backwards at her humor.

"Girls ... please get back to work. Let's not tease others as to avoid hurting feelings. Work diligently to get your sculptures done."

Juanita pretended to tremble at the command, but Cali knew she would team up with her buddies, including Eliza, to torment her later on the bus. Look what that bug had done!

CHAPTER 4

Somehow, Cali managed to survive the rest of art class. She had no appetite for lunch. Her father would want her to eat it anyway, though. He always told her how valuable food was and he said not to waste it — that strong, confident man who always made everyone around him feel safe.

The walk to the cafeteria seemed like a 5k race, but finally, the shouting, arguing, and chomping of the cafeteria could be heard. Cali sat in her seat at the girl's table for her class. That seat was the one that spun around and squeaked. Other times, Cali had found it amusing to play around with it, but today she didn't want to be heard. She unpacked her lettuce and tomato sandwich in silence.

It really did make it worse at lunch that she was sitting next to Mandy and Karina, the other girls in Eliza's sinister clique. Cali had tried just ignoring them other days to hopefully fulfill the "I'll ignore you and you'll ignore me" rule, but her half of the "promise" was the only one kept. Mandy and Karina always had a way to get onto the deepest of Cali's nerves and confidence.

Lunch had gone fine, though, until Karina broke into a curdling scream. Although Cali was careful not to daydream during lunch and focus on her food, she still felt as if she'd been awakened.

"An ant! An ant! Augh! Get it AWAY!" Karina yelped, jumping out of her seat across from Cali.

Cali took her eyes off of a potato chip to see a small black ant crawling in the middle of the table in front of Karina. She winced at the thought of another animal being killed by the girls in her class.

"Kill it!" shouted Mandy, her long black hair swishing to the side as she faced Cali.

"Ew! A bug! Get rid of it!" yelled Lindsay who hated bugs. She much preferred dogs, which was all she talked about.

"Squish it! What's wrong with you?!" asked Juanita who sat at the end of the table.

Soon the whole table of girls broke into chant — "Squish it, Cali! Kill it!"

"NO!" Cali finally spoke. She felt like she was going to throw up. Everyone was ganging up on her, and she wasn't about to kill an innocent ant! She finished her potato chips and used the bag they were in to capture the ant so it could be put outside where it would live and be safe.

"Cali! Why are you doing that? Just smoosh it and you'll be done!" announced Whitney.

"Yeah! You're stupid!" all the girls yelled in harmony.

Cali finally managed to put the ant on the bag, where it happily crawled. It was a hard struggle, with hands all over trying to kill the insect. She calmly raised her hand for a lunch lady to come over to put it outside. One came and obeyed, saving the ant from near death, to Cali's great relief.

"That was pathetic," Mandy muttered, moving to the opposite side of the table with everyone else to avoid Cali.

She just wanted to cry. Why was everyone so against her?

Just then, Sophie walked over to Cali. Sophie was in another class and never talked to her much, but she wasn't ever mean.

"I heard about the "incident"," she said, giggling, and then walked away.

How did everyone hear about her simple act of putting an ant outside so fast? What's wrong with that? All Cali knew was that it was certainly better than killing it!

CHAPTER 5

The rest of the day seemed like a spiral of loneliness. Of course, Cali was always lonely in the sense that no one would talk to her or had time to, but after lunch, it seemed like everyone was trying to avoid her. This happened often though, and after a day, it would all blow over.

This time, however, Cali seemed lonelier, because there was someone that was on her mind — Bug!

She raced off the bus, and opening the door to her house, her hand almost couldn't turn the knob. Her mother and Caius were in the living room down the hall, and to Cali's content, they didn't notice her excitement, and because Cali wasn't usually (really never) excited, that would have led to a question, which would have led to the discovery of Bug. One of the hard parts of keeping Bug was having it not be discovered — but of course, that was the exciting part, too.

Cali quietly closed the door to her bedroom. It was isolated from everything since it was in the very back of the house. The only way to get to it was through her father's entertainment room, and of course, for emotional reasons, no one wanted to go in there. Cali had always pleaded with her mom not to make her pass her father's room every day, for when she saw his special couch, it made her cry, but her request was denied. Plus, Cali had learned to hold in her tears. The room being in that spot now was perfect.

As if a zombie, she was led to Bug's home. The sponge had dried up, the pencil had tipped over, and Bug was in the exact same spot she left him in — the far right corner. Cali poked him to see if he was dead. His left antenna twitched. It was all ok. Cali was lucky he hadn't died, since there wasn't any food for him to eat.

Pinecones! Why did Bug have to be so picky to eat only pinecones?! Who could find a pinecone under an almost dead conifer in winter? Cali decided to rephrase her question to herself. Who would need to find a pinecone under an almost dead conifer in winter? The answer, she sighed, was her. She had given herself the responsibility to take care of this insect, and she wouldn't give up on it. She just wouldn't give up on the only important thing she had to do these days. The only thing that seemed to have any meaning anyway. Her math worksheet for homework would just have to wait.

Cali turned away from the western conifer seed beetle and headed out of her room to the living room. She was a bit nervous to talk to her mother, since she hadn't in three days. She knew that wasn't right, and she should be more social with her family, but Mrs. Still had been depressed lately about her husband being so far away in Afghanistan and having to take care of two kids all by herself. Meals were silent, and her mom was too busy with Caius going to school to kiss her daughter goodbye. Cali wondered why that little brat Caius got more attention.

When Cali entered the bright living room, scattered with toys and junk, Caius stopped laughing and Mrs. Still dropped a Lego.

"Mom, can I go outside?" Cali asked, sweat dripping down her forehead.

"Sure dear, just bundle up, and please don't stay out too long. I'll need help preparing dinner," her mother answered, her short, tangled hair flopping into her weary eyes.

Cali was too busy with her problems to think of her mother's, but she noticed her let — down appearance anyway.

She galloped out the door into her small backyard, the front yard of the neighbor behind her. In Ashford, the peeling, small country houses seem to pile up on one another, with the exception when someone owns a farm.

In the shared yard, a small, dying or maybe already dead pine tree stood. Nobody ever bothered to cut it down. About half of the branches were missing, and it was only a couple of feet taller than Cali. She couldn't remember it ever bearing pinecones, but this was the only conifer she had, and for Bug, it was worth a shot.

It was a freezing January this year, so Cali fingered each branch, searching it for spiky growths with fuzzy pink gloves — no pinecone here, no pinecone there, no pinecone anywhere!

When she was just about to go inside for dinner, at the way back of the tree on the very top, there was a huge, chocolate-colored pinecone, hidden by branches and dusted with snow. Cali saw a squirrel nestled in the branches up top, eyeing the pinecone, too. She had to be the first one to get it, but the branches of the tree were dying, thin, and hard to climb.

Cali carefully placed her foot on the bottom branch of the tree, nearest to the trunk since that's the thickest part. She watched the small squirrel with one eye, and the pinecone in the other. Her hand grasped a branch higher up, but it quickly snapped, throwing Cali off balance and making her step off the branch. She got back on, to see the squirrel was scared away. Now she only needed to reach the pinecone just a few feet up!

She moved ever so slowly, analyzing every branch she put her weight on, as not to snap one and fall off. Within a few branches, Cali could almost reach the pinecone. It glistened beautifully with melted snow, and Cali could just see Bug happily gobbling it down.

Cali reached cautiously for the pinecone, pushing her weight harder onto the branch below her feet to get just a few inches higher. Almost ... almost ... SNAP! The branch below Cali's feet crumbled under her weight, sending Cali and the pinecone that was shaken off the tree, three feet to the ground.

Spiky branches poked and prodded Cali all the way down, tearing her new jacket and scratching her face. The delicate pinecone was stuck on a branch up high, and Cali didn't want to bother going back up again, since she had to help her mother with dinner.

She sighed, nearing the door, and kicking the snow. "Huh?" Cali asked to herself. She had kicked something small and hard, and it wasn't a piece of ice. It was a baby pinecone, about ¼ the size of the other one. She supposed it would do anyway.

CHAPTER 6

Cali went back into the house and dropped the pinecone in her room. She placed it right beside Bug, who still hadn't moved. Would it even appreciate all of her work? Probably not. What a small pinecone she'd found.

"Cali ... where were you? I need you to help me make the pizza. I'll do the crust, you do the sauce," Mrs. Still said from the kitchen.

Homemade Pizza was a comfort food for the Stills. They used to have it every Friday when Mr. Still was around, but when he left, it was only eaten when he was missed most. Cali liked making the warm sauce, because it made her feel like she was being hugged by her dad when she ate it — that warm, big, bear hug. Her mom liked the crust, since she thought that when she made a hard crust, her husband would stay strong.

While they were making the dish, it seemed awkwardly quiet, so Mrs. Still began some small talk. "Cali, why'd you go outside?" she asked as she lugged the flour back to the cabinet.

Cali froze in her tracks when she was taking spices out. She couldn't let her mom find out about Bug and how she had to get a pinecone for it ... but she had other reasons for going outside.

When her dad had first left for Afghanistan, the outside was like a sanctuary and a school for her. She watched squirrels scurry up trees, learning from them how to run away from bullies like crows. She'd watch bushes every day, seeing how each day she watched them, their flowers grew bigger and their branches grew stronger. She hoped, that just like a bush, she'd grow as quickly. Most of all, she'd eyed all of the bugs under rocks and crawling up trees. She loved them most, because they never left her.

"I like it outside," Cali said, steering away from Bug, yet still being truthful.

"Wasn't it cold, though?"

Cali thought about that, too. Winter was her favorite time of year! It was the time you could see miles through the trees and the air tasted like premium honey made by the busiest of bees. Besides, being cold and alone was what she was all the time now. She'd gotten used to it, and she'd found ways to find the warmth in situations.

"Mom, I don't mind the cold. I look forward to going inside, when I get the warmest of warm, much warmer than I'd ever feel if I hadn't gone outside in the first place."

The girls worked a bit longer.

"Cali, that's very insightful," Mrs. Still said finally.

Cali grinned a faint smile. That had been one of the first times in a while that someone had made her feel good inside.

Outside the window, they heard the confident humming of the mail truck as it passed their mailbox, sticking the daily bills and unwanted magazines into their mailbox, which was peeling and crooked by about 45°.

"Could you be a dear and get the mail?" asked Mrs. Still as she kneaded the dough between her palms.

Cali quickly washed off her hands, slipped on a coat, and headed out the door along the stone path to the mailbox. She hurriedly unloaded the mail, skimming through the junk letters before bringing it back. Nothing, nothing, huh?

Cali threw the junk on the floor of the entryway of her house and brought the strange letter to her mom.

Mrs. Still slowly tore it open and started to cry.

"What mom, what?!" asked Cali, concerned.

Her mom took her into her arms and kissed Cali on the top of her head. "He's coming home! Your daddy's coming home early, Cali! In just 2 weeks we'll see him again!" she cried happily. "He's coming a whole week before his birthday to be here even longer with us!"

Cali couldn't fully appreciate this amazing moment as her mom was. This meant Bug had to be kept extra secret. She didn't quite know whether to be happy or sad — maybe neutral, like always, would be best.

That night, though, the pizza tasted even better than normal, and everyone had that warm feeling without even going outside first.

CHAPTER 7

After brushing her teeth, Cali quickly closed the door to her room. She pulled down the shades on her one small window. Then, she ran to Bug's home.

Bug had moved to the other end of the box and was slowly making its way back around — that was good. The sponge looked dryer than ever, and the pinecone that she had gone to so much trouble for was just sitting there. Cali analyzed it very closely to see if Bug had taken any bite out of it. Can it even bite? She could have sworn there was a very small hole on the bottom, about the size of the head of a moisture ant. At least she hoped that was what she saw.

Cali's homework was fractions — again. It wasn't that she hated fractions. She was bored of them. Not many knew, but when Cali knew something, she knew it. All of the teachers put her in the "slow" group because she was a slow learner. She never caught onto things fast like some of the other kids. She needed the task to be explained in many different ways for her to get it, but then she really understood and could do whatever it was, be it fractions or limericks, even better than the higher level kids. Yet she was still thought of as "dumb". Dumb, boring, messy, and quiet was what she was. At least that was what people thought of her.

¼ x 2/7= ... Cali stared down at the paper. She didn't want to do it. She peered over her desk at Bug. It had crawled to the back of the box and was still determined, crawling all around.

Bug ... all it did was crawl around. Bug was just as boring as the fractions. Ho Hum! Everything was boring!

Now Bug had made its way slowly but steadily onto the small sponge. Was Bug thirsty? Boring or not, Cali couldn't deprive an animal of water, since that would be just plain mean. Cali quickly took the sponge out and, steering clear of her mom, headed to the kitchen to dampen the sponge for Bug. She grinned as she headed back to her room, since she got out of doing fractions, and was feeding an animal.

Her smile soon faded, though, when she found the door open.

"Cali, what's this?" She heard in a high, squeaky voice. That was the voice of Caius, as he pointed at Bug's home!

Cali immediately slammed the door behind her and shoved her hand over her brother's mouth, smooshing in his pudgy little cheeks.

"Aren't you supposed to be playing with Mom, Caius?" Cali hissed.

She really never talked with her brother. Ever since he was born, Cali had been extremely jealous, and she hated how much everyone loved him and never her.

"Mmf!" yelled Caius, pushing Cali's hand off of his mouth and frowning. "What'd you do that for?" he whined.

Caius always whined. That was how he got what he wanted. And he always got what he wanted.

"Tell me what's in the box!!" he yelled, about to start one of his tantrums.

"Ssh!" whispered Cali. "Be quiet, nobody's supposed to know!"

"Tell me!" whispered Caius — at least he tried to whisper. He couldn't reach Cali's dresser, so he couldn't see Bug inside the box.

"No! Why were you in my room in the first place?!" asked Cali, bending down so she was level with her little brother.

"Mommy was washing the dishes and couldn't read me a story, so I wanted you to!"

"Well, you don't just go into someone else's room without asking them. Now go!" Cali never liked being in the same room as Caius. He stressed her out.

Caius looked as if he was about to do one of his fake cries. "I just want to hear <u>Captain Tough Saves Miss Patterson</u>!" he cried. Caius was also good at crying whenever he wanted to.

"Fine, Caius. You win. I'll read you the story if you get out of my room and never come back in." Cali smirked.

"Thank you! You're the best sister ever!" Caius grinned, automatically stopping crying.

"All right, I'll go get the book from your bookcase. Stay put," Cali said, leading Caius into their father's entertainment room and closing the door to her room as she walked to get Caius's favorite story. She had made a perfect compromise! That was close one!

As she walked back to her room, Caius was nowhere to be found in the entertainment room. Cali walked to the small hallway that led to her room from the entertainment room, but he wasn't there either. Even worse, the door to her room was open.

Cali ran inside to find Caius standing on her desk chair, staring right into Bug's home and reaching his hand inside through the plastic wrap! She threw the book on the ground and snatched up the box that was so dear to her.

"What's wrong with you Caius?!" Cali fumed. "We made a compromise!"

Caius started his fake crying again and his puffy cheeks went red to make him look innocent, but Cali could see him smirking under his fake emotion.

"I'm not falling for it, Caius. Don't touch my stuff, do you hear me?" Cali peered into the box to make sure Bug was ok. It was frozen stiff on the sponge. "I'll get you for this. I'm NOT reading you the story."

Caius stopped crying when he saw that he wouldn't get away with his act.

"Are you sure I won't get *you*?" He grinned. "I know you have a bug, Cali. Daddy's coming, and he told me how he doesn't want you to have any bugs. I'm gonna tell mom, and she'll squish the bug and make you grounded."

Caius was so spoiled, and whenever he didn't get what he wanted, he made you pay — big time. He was a sly little boy.

"Caius, please don't tell! I love this bug! I can't have it killed!" Cali didn't really love the bug. She just loved keeping it safe and knowing that she was saving it.

"Well," Caius sneered. "Maybe if you do something for me, I won't tell."

"It's a deal! Yes! I'll do it! Just name it!" Cali blurted out, staring at Bug, who had not moved because of the commotion.

"You have to be my personal butler for a week!" Caius laughed.

"No, Caius! You can do your own chores! I have my own things to do!" Cali argued.

Caius started running out the door. "Mom, I've got something to tell you!" he said.

"No!" Cali rushed after him into the kitchen, where Mrs. Still was still washing dishes. "I'll do it," Cali whispered into his ear at the last moment, thinking of Bug.

"What, dear?" their mom asked.

Cali glared at Caius. He stared back at her, confirming the agreement. "Cali read me a story," he said.

"That's nice, dear," Mrs. Still said.

CHAPTER 8

"Cali!" Caius screeched in Cali's face.

Cali was still in her bed in the morning. She didn't want to get out. She hoped a day had skipped and it was Saturday. Or maybe even a week and it was next Friday. If she had slept a week, she would've slept through being Caius's personal butler. It'd be annoying, but how much harm could a 6-year-old do, anyway? She could make it through the week.

"Get out of my room!" Cali commanded, sleepiness obvious in her voice. She flopped out of bed and pushed her brother, who was still in his pajamas.

"Ah ah ah! You're my personal butler! I came to tell you that you have to follow me around all day, obeying my every command! You can go to school, but otherwise, you have to be with ME!"

"Whoopee," Cali muttered under her breath.

"Ah ah ah! Butlers aren't allowed to be sarcastic! They're like yes — men. Now come along and dress. Then come into my room and pick out clothes for me!"

Cali sneered at Caius. "You can do all of that yourself! You're a big boy!"

"Ah ah ..." Cali broke in before Caius could say his last "ah".

"Yes, master. I'll do just that." Cali put on her largest fake smile and shoved Caius out of her room.

She quickly dressed and was about to head out when she eyed the clock. It was 4:00, still the middle of the night! What was Caius doing waking her up so early?! Then Cali eyed Bug, and you should've seen it go!

Bug was zooming across the box. Usually, Bug was just sitting in one spot, but now it was completely active!

Bug sped up the side of the box, so high you could see its antennae poking out. It would surely escape! The plastic wrap had broken!

Cali thumbed all around her room for a new cover to the box, anything to keep Bug from escaping, which was obviously nocturnal.

Book? Too thick. Old t-shirt? No holes. Finally, Cali came to a three-holed piece of paper. The holes were small enough for her insect not to get through but large enough for it to breathe. The paper also let in light, so Cali could look in at Bug. Perfect!

By the time Cali got the tape to attach the paper to the box, Bug was crawling down the side at a fast pace! If it got loose, her mom could find out about it, or worse, somebody wouldn't see it on the ground and it'd get stepped on!

Cali dropped the paper and roll of tape, sticking her hand on her dresser, below Bug. It crawled onto her hand, tickling her small palm. Cali stared down at Bug. Its antennae whirled and twirled as it moved, as though it were playing the drums on Cali's hand. The antennae softly brushed against her hand whenever it moved.

She couldn't help but giggle at the tickling insect on her finger. She smiled. The last time she smiled was when she first found Bug! Her passion for animals was strong once more! Nobody could ruin this, not even Caius! She'd keep Bug a secret until she could let it go!

Cali finally snapped back into reality, carefully placing Bug back into the box and taping the cover on.

"Now you're safe!" she whispered into one of the holes.

As Cali walked out of her room, she found Caius running up in front of her, with his clothes on.

"I see you picked out your own clothes since you're completely capable of that task," Cali smirked.

"Yeah. I got bored. I'll let it slide this time. Where were you? Does it take you THAT LONG to dress?" Caius asked.

"I had some business to take care of, ok?" Cali was still very tired. They should still be sleeping!

"Fine!

"Make me breakfast! I want an early start to the day so you can do lots of chores for me!" said Caius, folding his arms.

"Can we just go back to bed? Let's try this again at 7:00."

CHAPTER 9

Caius was back in Cali's room at 7:03. Mrs. Still had already made breakfast buttered toast for breakfast, and Caius pleaded with her to make Cali prepare it tomorrow.

He forced Cali to brush his hair, brush his teeth, and make his bed. Their mom had no problem with Cali doing that, for it was usually she that would complete those tasks for Caius. She was quite a sucker for him. She still thought of him as her baby. Cali was just "the other one".

Cali went to school early at 7:30, to navigate around Caius's unneeded commands and the rush of the halls in school.

She beat everyone to class to get a head start on her work. Nobody could disturb her while she was doing work, or her teacher, Mrs. Graham, would get upset. Mrs. Graham was a very quiet teacher, but if anyone was mean to one another or disturbed someone else, she really took charge. She never taught big lessons, but made her children read the lesson in some kind of anthology instead.

For Cali, that was a much better way to learn. She could teach and think for herself. If she didn't understand something at first, she could read the paragraph over, but you couldn't make your teacher repeat a whole paragraph, if the teaching was oral.

Of course, other students objected to this style of teaching. They could understand better and concentrate on something if it was said aloud.

Cali began on reading the next math lesson. Mrs. Graham had allowed her into the classroom early as long as she worked diligently and did only the math lesson.

Lesson 17: Perimeter, Area, and Volume — Measuring Your Shapes. Perimeter is the area around a shape. To find the perimeter, add up the lengths of the sides of a figure. As Cali was taking that in, the wave of children from the buses spluttered into the classroom. Cali was usually stuck in that rush. She was only a block away from the school, though. She could walk easily. She loved being in the snow — though it was dirty now, and didn't mind walking in the cold.

Area is the space inside a shape. To get the area of a rectangle, multiply the length x width of the figure. For triangles, do the base x height then divide by 2. For parallelograms ... Cali looked up to find everyone at their desks. Everyone had their math books open. Everyone had their eyes on perimeter, area, and volume. Nobody was snickering at her! Phew! Nobody cared about the ant incident anymore!

Out of pure happiness, Cali started daydreaming about Bug. It crawled around, tickling her finger. Then, she thought of Caius, and being his butler — ugh! Thinking of that made her look up to the orderly room. Everyone was working hard. Mrs. Graham was grading papers — wait, Mrs. Graham wasn't grading papers! A thin, black-haired girl with an orange dress and colorful socks was talking to her.

Mrs. Graham finally walked to the front of the room. She only did that to tell the students what subject to work on.

"Class, we have a new student! Her name is Inez. Cali, would you show her around the school?"

Cali couldn't refuse, so she went to the front of the room and brought Inez out of the classroom.

Inez smiled brightly at Cali.

That smile made Cali smile, too. This Inez seemed like a nice girl! "Promise you won't listen to what other people in the class say about me!" Cali told Inez as they walked down the hall.

"I won't. Why? You seem nice! Don't people like you — Cali, right?!" Inez asked, her dress billowing.

"Um, they just discriminate. Let's go to the arts room."

CHAPTER 10

"So your music room and art room are combined?" asked Inez.

"Yep. The art teacher thinks music helps people think creatively, so there you go," answered Cali.

"That's a great idea! You know, I play the flute. Maybe I could inspire some art with it!"

Cali giggled. She showed Inez around the whole school — the gym, the auditorium, the cafeteria, even the library.

"Your school is so fancy!" Inez commented.

"Why, where'd you used to go?"

Inez sighed. "I went to Linden Valley Elementary School in Nevada, and they were really mean there. I pleaded with my mom to move somewhere else and we came here. So far, people are really nice. It is SO much better than Nevada!"

Cali wondered if Inez would be bullied here as she was in Nevada. She didn't want Inez to leave. She was her only friend besides Bug! Inez seemed like a cool and nice girl. Cali was confident that Inez wouldn't get bullied, and they could stay friends forever.

The girls walked back to the classroom, laughing all the way. Inez sat next to Cali, and the day passed very quickly. They were always together, and nobody bothered them whatsoever! Cali even forgot about Bug — for a tiny split second that is, but Bug was only in the back of Cali's mind.

"Cali, can I come over to your house this afternoon? My house is really noisy because they're still doing work on it before we can fully move in," Inez asked as they walked down the hallway that afternoon.

Nobody had EVER asked Cali if they could come over to her house. It was a breakthrough! It was incredible! She had to say YES!

Then Cali remembered about annoying little Caius and being his butler. Would he tell on her about keeping Bug if she didn't do his chores? And would her mom be mad if Cali brought over somebody without asking? She already had enough work to do. Cali didn't want to make her mother stressed. Her father always said not to stress people. That man with eyes that sparkled like diamonds when he smiled. Cali also couldn't forget about Bug! She had to change its pinecones and wet its sponge. Would inviting Inez over really be a good idea?

Though Cali's mind said "NO!", her vocal chords and mouth didn't quite get the message. "Sure, of course you can come over! How about 3:30?" she blurted out.

She felt like hitting herself on the head. Though she truly wanted Inez to hang out with her at her house, that was definitely the worse and thoughtless decision. This could mean big trouble!

"Oh, thank you, Cali! I love this place!" Inez grinned, and they departed onto their separate buses.

On the bus, Cali didn't quite know whether to frown or smile. She'd made a new friend but would be betraying everyone else. Maybe Bug could help.

Cali walked off the bus timidly, thinking the door to her house was poisonous and would bite her. The inside would probably be the fiery molten core of a volcano. Cali hoped she wouldn't trip and fall inside.

CHAPTER 11

When Cali walked through the door to her house, it seemed like she was being pounced on. Caius ran up to her to tell her what chores he wanted done. Her mom ran up to her, too, but Cali realized she was only just trying to pull Caius away to stuff in a few more minutes of mother — son bonding time before she had to make dinner, trying to please two kids with the few ingredients they could afford.

Cali felt as if she could barely breathe with everyone in front of her like that. Everyone was staring at her, and she began to feel claustrophobic.

"Cali, make me ice water with lemon," Caius commanded.

"I'll do that, but how about we finish our game of action heroes! Sorry, luv," Mrs. Still said to Cali.

"Thanks Mom ... for taking Caius off my hands ... oh, and ..." Cali searched for the right words.

"What dear?" her mom asked patiently.

"Um, I invited my new friend over," Cali whispered in her softest voice, which was very soft.

"That's great!"

"NO!" yelled Caius. "You have to be my butler!"

Cali was glad her mother approved of Inez coming over, but Caius — he'd surely tell!

"Caius, Cali doesn't have to be your butler. This is her first friend since preschool!" Mrs. Still said, patting Caius on the head lovingly.

Cali remembered her old friend, Yasmin. They shared a bond of bugs and cookies. Nobody was very intelligent in preschool. When they saw something move, they squished it, thinking it was funny. Yasmin and Cali thought the little ants intruding in their classroom were cute. She was the first and only person Cali met who shared her interest in insects. The girls soon became easy best friends, always coloring together and sharing their chocolate chip cookies.

Yasmin came from Iran, but after she was born, things were heating up in the Middle East. They decided to come to America, which seemed safer.

Since Yasmin was so young when she moved to America, she didn't have an accent, but Cali always loved the sound of her mom talking when she came to the preschool to help. Cali loved accents, especially English accents. They sounded so elegant and fancy.

Cali and Yasmin were inseparable until the summer before kindergarten. Yasmin usually did the talking. Cali was more of a listener, and one day, when Yasmin was telling Cali about the beaches in Iran, she blurted out that she was moving.

Cali thought she must have heard wrong: her best friend going across the ocean — that couldn't be true!

But it was, and in two weeks, the week before kindergarten started, she was gone. Off on a plane to a scary place. Things had cleared up for a while, and her parents took the opportunity to go back to their country.

Before Yasmin left, she gave Cali a giant ant she found in her backyard. Cali promised she'd cherish the ant, but since Cali loved nature, she knew she couldn't keep it. She let the ant go the next day, and she also let go of Yasmin. Yasmin was the only person she interacted with in preschool, the only one that she talked to. Every other toddler socialized with everyone, so when Yasmin left, Cali was all alone.

In kindergarten, she also found out that people made fun of her and Yasmin behind their backs. They thought they were weird for playing with bugs, so for the rest of her life so far, she had no friends and was teased.

Cali snapped back into reality. Caius was glaring at her through narrow eyes.

"Cali, you're not obeying me! I'm gonna tell!"

"Tell what, dear?" Mrs. Still asked.

Cali felt her face getting hot, her breath tensing. She stared Caius straight in the eyes, scared, angry.

"Fine, Caius — um, when Inez is over, we can do chores for you!" Cali blurted out, desperate to keep Bug.

"Ooo! Two butlers! Mommy, I have nothing to say!" Caius said, grinning mischievously.

Mrs. Still looked at her children suspiciously but then just rolled her eyes and sighed. Cali and Caius could be strange sometimes. She went back to doing the dishes as Cali frowned at Caius. She had an evil little brother.

CHAPTER 12

As Cali was sorting Caius's socks, the doorbell rang. "Be right back, Caius. You'll have two helpers to sort your "winter socks" soon."

Cali fixed her hair as she ran to the front door. She grinned as she turned the knob.

"Hi, Cali!" Inez cheerfully said as she walked into the Still's house. She eyed the entrance room, gazing at the plants in the doorway.

"Your house and your lawn are so big! Your neighbors are like ten feet away!" said Inez.

"Um, actually, we have a pretty small yard," Cali said, surprised at Inez.

"Well, I lived in Henderson, Nevada. Everyone was so close together. I needed some personal space!"

Cali stepped a few feet away from Inez, not wanting her to get intimidated and move away.

"So what should we do?!" Inez was back to her cheery self.

Cali would probably take her to the family room and play Scrabble with her (if friends even liked to play Scrabble, Cali didn't have a friend in so long that she didn't know) ... if her little brother wasn't waiting for his socks to be sorted, and his hair to be brushed, and this and that done. Cali looked down at her feet before meeting Inez's eyes.

"Er, before we do anything, do you want to meet my brother?" Cali asked, wondering if Caius would let them play if she asked him. He might say yes — might.

"Oh, yes! Cali, I'm so glad I made friends so quickly here! You've been so kind to me!"

With that, Cali felt a pang of guilt. She couldn't make her brand new friend, one that actually liked her, sort her brother's socks! But Bug would die if her mom found out about it from Caius. Suddenly, Cali wanted to feel that tickling sensation of Bug crawling on her.

Cali brought Inez to Caius's room and quickly introduced them before Caius could butt in.

"Inez, this is Caius," Cali said, smiling awkwardly.

"I'm pleased to meet you, Caius! You're so cute! How old are you?" asked Inez, grinning.

"Six," Caius replied, blushing at the attention. He just LOVED when people called him cute.

Cali walked over to Caius and whispered in his ear. "See how nice my friend is? You'll ruin our friendship if you make her do your chores! You're not supposed to do your friend's brother's chores when you go to their house! Please just let me do things with her before I do any more chores! Please!"

Caius took some time to ponder the decision. Inez walked over to Cali, wondering what was going on.

"Cali, can I see your room now? Can we play a game? Do you have Scrabble? I just can't get enough of it!"

"NO!" Caius blurted out.

"What? What's wrong?" Inez asked, looking concerned.

"Nothing," said Cali, escorting Inez out of Caius's room.

"Stop!" Caius yelled. "You OWE me, Cali. I'm telling!"

"NO!" Cali exclaimed.

"What's wrong?" Inez asked. "Is it me? Oh, I'll just leave. I knew I couldn't find an awesome friend this fast — it's just my luck."

Inez began to leave the room.

"Stop!" Cali screamed. Bug was the source of all of her problems!

"Caius, please! I'll do work in the middle of the night if you let me play with Inez. Please!"

"Fine," Caius said under his breath and plopped down on his bed.

"C'mon, Inez. Let's go play Scrabble!" Cali said, smiling once more. She expected Inez to be smiling broadly, too.

"Um, I don't know, Cali. You're acting really weird now. I don't think you want me here, and I don't know if you even want to be my friend. I DO know you have to sort something out with your brother. May I use the phone? I need to call my mom to go home," Inez said, frowning.

Cali didn't even bother stopping her. She ran to Bug in her room. Her life was ruined again.

CHAPTER 13

Cali quickly pulled off the paper on Bug's box. She let Bug crawl slowly onto her finger. It didn't. This was the afternoon, so Cali should've known Bug would be slow. She wanted to hurt Bug for doing this to her. She couldn't hurt Bug — that would be wrong. Maybe she'd just put it outside in the snow and let nature hurt it. Then maybe she could get things back to normal. Best of all, she wouldn't have to be Caius's butler!

She could get Inez back as her best friend. She'd only had a best friend once, and she loved how it felt. Having someone always watching your back made you feel loved. Having someone who always wanted to be with you made you feel wanted. Having a loyal and compassionate friend who made you laugh and was always by your side was the best feeling in the world! If Cali could just get that feeling back, would it matter if one insect died in the snow? No. Would anyone care if her secret bug were gone one day? No, because they hadn't known about it anyway, except for Caius, of course. This was the perfect plan! Maybe Cali could get her life working properly! Maybe she'd even GET a life!

Cali was just about to pick Bug up and take it outside (an easy task, since Bug wasn't moving at all), when it moved a single antennae.

What was that supposed to mean? Why did it all of a sudden make a move as she gently picked it up? Did she hurt it accidentally? Cali hoped not.

In her hand, Bug moved once more. It took a step closer to her wrist. A small, yet dignified step.

Cali stared at Bug, who wouldn't usually be moving at this hour. Why was it using up so much energy just to be sent outside to die?

She made sure the coast was clear before going out her door. Caius, by the noises he was making, was scheming up something evil to do to her in his room. And her mom was still out in the garage working on her car that was near dead, to be productive AND stay out of the way of her daughter and her new friend. That was Cali's idea.

All of a sudden, Bug scampered frantically across her palm, making Cali giggle slightly.

Cali went into a daze. That feeling of Bug on her skin was a feeling of no other, better than the feeling of friendship. Better than everything, the feeling of insects — small creatures — amazing creatures that too many take for granted. Those tickly things that people squash and think are pesky, but really make the world go round. Cali loved that feeling. She wanted to keep Bug. She never wanted to kill it! Never! She quickly placed Bug back in its box, grinning at her little insect.

She sat on her bed. That feeling of insects was great, but the feeling of friendship was pretty good as well. Why couldn't Cali have both? Why? Nothing was holding her back!

Cali could keep her plan from before, but without the killing Bug part. She'd just TELL Caius it was dead, so she wouldn't have to be his butler anymore and also so he won't bug her anymore. Then she could have Inez over and make up with her!

It was brilliant! The only hard part was hiding Bug enough so nobody would find it again. Nobody would have to know except her. Nobody could pull her away from a perfect life! Not even that dad of hers. He wouldn't have to know she was keeping a secret western conifer seed bug in her room! All he'd see was a happy daughter!

CHAPTER 14

Cali grinned to herself at her smart plan. Where to hide Bug? Under her bed — no, Cali couldn't fit under there so she wouldn't be able to access Bug easily or at all. Behind her pillow — no, that would suffocate it. Suddenly Cali had a great idea. She didn't have to hide it at all! She could just disguise it!

She got some brown paper out of her art supplies drawer in her closet and with a white crayon, wrote "Cali's Jewelry Box". She taped the paper on Bug's box, but left the three-holed paper on the top so Bug could breathe. If Caius broke their pact and came into her room, he wouldn't dare touch a jewelry box. He was a little boy, so he hated looking at girly jewelry.

She strolled to Caius, who was in his room. When he saw her, he ran to her, jabbering about chores and tasks to be done.

"Hey, Caius. I don't have to be your butler anymore. Sorry, but you've got to do your own chores now." Cali said, grinning as she did.

"No! I'm going to tell Mommy about your little bug! You'll get in BIG trouble unless you make me a snack right now!" Caius argued, standing on his bed to reach Cali's height.

"Oh, but it wouldn't matter anymore if you told Mother I had a pet invertebrate — because I don't." Cali shuddered as the horrible words came out of her mouth. "My bug is dead."

"Oh," Caius said, sighing. "I'm sorry to hear that."

Cali walked out of his room to hers, smiling. She'd done it! He believed that she had no insect. Now she could go on with her life in peace.

When Caius sighed, he definitely didn't feel bad about the bug. He felt bad about himself, not getting free work. Yep, that was her sinister brother!

Ok, she'd sorted out things with Caius, but now she had to sort out her problems with Inez.

Cali scuttled nervously to the phone. Her fingers couldn't find the buttons to press. The phone's ringing made her ears ring and her head pound. Inez seemed really mad earlier. Could she convince her that she didn't have any more problems with her brother? Could she get her one and only friend back?

When Cali heard Inez's voice, her head beat faster, like a hummingbird flapping its wings on a drum.

Cali hoped her questions would be answered with yeses. Yes, Inez would be convinced that Cali didn't have any more problems with her brother. Yes, Inez would be her friend again, but when Cali explained that her brother wouldn't butt in anymore and they could be friends again, all Inez said was "No" and "I'm busy".

She couldn't understand why such a cheerful, wonderful girl wouldn't forgive her. It was such a small situation, too! All that happened was Cali ignored Inez for a teensy bit, just to sort a teensy (maybe a little bigger) situation out with Caius.

"What, why? I didn't do anything. I only had a little dilemma with my brother. You were the one who didn't want to play Scrabble!" Cali demanded, confused with Inez.

"Well, it's not just about what happened 20 minutes ago. I may have gotten a little too mad about you and your brother since I don't have siblings, but I saw that you didn't want to be with me. I found someone else who wants to be with me. She invited me to her house 15 minutes ago, and that's where I am right now. Her name is Mandy!" Inez said, with a light, snobby tone.

"Mandy?! She's so mean! She does NOT want to be with you! She just wants to tear you up! Don't hang out with her, Inez! Hang out with me!"

The phone paused and Cali heard Mandy and Inez laughing in the background before Inez spoke again.

"Oh, Cali. You should know that *you* were the one who was going to tear me up! Mandy told me all about you! She's a wonderful person by the way and has an extremely neat house!"

"What did she tell you?! It's wrong, Inez! Believe me, whatever she said is all wrong!" Cali yelled.

"She told me you had no friends because you were really dumb and couldn't even do simple math problems; also, because you never talked and just daydreamed. I mean, I heard you talk, but Mandy told me that you rarely talk. She also told me you're really into bugs and always pick them up and play with them. That's just gross, and I think keeping animals captive is very mean. That's against my beliefs. Oh, and when you said not to listen to the other girls, you should know they've been the nice ones to me, and you've just been what they said —weird. "

A tear rolled down Cali's cheek. Inez was her first chance at a best friend. Her first chance at sanity. Her first chance at a real life.

Cali hung up, imagining Inez directing her glorious smile to those who have only sinister stares. There was nothing wrong with Cali. There was nothing wrong with keeping bugs in a little "jewelry box" in your room until winter blows over. Or was there something wrong? That was certainly what everyone else thought.

CHAPTER 15

The weekend passed by quickly, since Cali didn't have any annoying chores to do. She mostly read and stared at Bug all day. Cali didn't sleep Sunday night, though. She didn't eat dinner either. She just stared at her "jewelry", since it was the time it shined the most. Cali couldn't understand why others didn't think it shined — why they didn't think she shined either. Was she really that dull? Or maybe she was just a diamond hidden very well in piles of heavy rubble.

The next morning Cali really didn't feel like going to school. School meant Inez, Mandy, and the rest of "the crew", as they called themselves. School meant embarrassment and teasing.

But, in order not to upset her father who wanted her to have a certain academic record, she went anyway. She told her mom she needed exercise and walked there early to avoid the bus. The bus just meant trouble.

She arrived at school one minute late, even though she lived close to the school. She didn't know what time to leave to get there on time. She got to the room during attendance, getting a "Tardy".

Cali slipped into her homeroom seat, directly in front of Mandy. She hoped out of sight would be out of mind. But Inez sat right next to her. Mrs. Graham saw them become friends when Cali showed Inez around the school so she thought that would be the best seating arrangement. Oh sure.

Inez and Mandy were leaning over and giggling with each other, pointing at Cali in the minute before class started where attendance was counted, even talking when Mrs. Graham started talking. Cali listened, though she should have been listening to their morning assignment. Since Mrs. Graham rarely taught but left the teaching to the books, she told the class everything they had to do in the day in their morning assignment.

"Did you see her room? Was it gross and weird?" Mandy whispered to Inez, being careful to act attentive whenever Mrs. Graham looked their way.

Inez was a good student, obviously trying to listen to the teacher. She passed a note to Mandy instead of talking. Who knows what it said?

"Girls, stop that! I see you talking and passing notes! You'll be in big trouble in a minute!" Mrs.

Graham yelled. She rarely yelled, but couldn't stand it when people weren't paying attention.

Cali grinned, almost wanting to laugh. Finally, those mean girls were going to get a taste of their own medicine! She looked over at Inez who had turned pale white rather than her usual creamy caramel complexion.

"I'll know if you girls were listening if you can repeat what I just said to the class. Cali, Inez, Mandy — tell me ... you first Cali," Mrs. Graham demanded, walking slowly closer to their desks.

Cali looked astonished. She didn't do anything! It was them!

"And yes, Cali, I saw you looking at your friend Inez!" Mrs. Graham told Cali.

She blushed, astounded. Was she really? She was listening and being a good student, while they were distracting her. Cali still couldn't quite recall half of the morning assignment. It wasn't her fault, though!

"Um, I'm sorry, Mrs. Graham, but when Inez was passing notes, she distracted me," Cali said quietly, seeing Inez shoot her a frown.

"Yes, but I know you, Cali. You're good at following rules. You can do better, although Inez may be a bad influence on you."

Inez looked heartbroken as Mrs. Graham said that. When Cali showed her around the school, she said she had been a top student in Nevada. She would always follow rules but couldn't stand the mean kids there.

"Now, Mandy, with your talking, I doubt you were listening."

"No, ma'am. You said to do math book pages 143-145 by the end of the day," Mandy confidently said.

Cali guessed she must have just listened to the teacher while Inez was writing her reply note.

"Good, Mandy. I guess Cali was the one near you who was talking. Maybe Inez, too. Inez, what did I say to do before math?" Mrs. Graham asked, adjusting her thin green glasses.

Inez's mouth fell limp. She had been writing her note as Mrs. Graham was recently talking. "Reading page 60?" she guessed.

"Cali and Inez, since you weren't listening to the morning assignments and now don't know what to do today, I'm afraid I'm going to have to send you to Mr. T's office. As for the rest of you, you may begin. I will alert you at music time, and by then, you should have your first 2 pages of science done," Mrs. Graham said in her calm, quiet voice. She scuttled over to her desk and began to do some kind of work that no student has identified before on her laptop as Cali walked out the classroom door, with Inez a few feet behind.

CHAPTER 16

Inez followed Cali down the hall silently. Cali occasionally looked back at her, but Inez turned her head, though Cali could see tears on her cheek. She wanted to cry, too. Her father would hate to hear this, but Cali was stronger than Inez was. Nobody knew, but after all of her teasing and loneliness, she'd developed a thick outer shell. It held in her feelings of sadness and her tears. The shell was like a barrier to the rest of the world, and it was very good at protecting Cali from it, even when she didn't want to be protected.

With Inez so sad, Cali finally decided to break the ice, even though Inez had betrayed her.

"I assume this is your first trip to the principal's office," Cali said quietly, stopping so Inez could catch up to her, but Inez stopped too, so they were both standing there in the middle of the main school hallway.

She nodded, sniffling.

"I've been to the principal's office before. It's not so bad. I went in first grade, and I was terrified, so I know how you feel, but you'll be ok." Cali tried to make Inez feel better — to make herself feel better. She wondered what her consequence would be.

"Mandy is so mean," Inez said.

Cali smiled at Inez's comment. Finally, she understood.

"If she's going to get me in trouble on my second day at a school, I don't want to be her friend."

In her head, Cali was dancing. Maybe Inez would want to be her friend again.

Inez saw Cali smiling. "I don't want to be your friend either, if you were wondering."

"Why? We had so much fun together! You liked me! You understood me! We were *friends*!" Cali's mouth tingled with the word. Calling somebody a friend was spectacular.

"Because ... I'm not quite sure how to put it to you gently. Hmm. You're not a happy person. You have too many problems. Plus, you're just so quiet. You have nothing to say for yourself, to show who you really are. People like Mandy make things up about you because you won't do anything about it and because they don't know who you really are. That's why they make up who you are. To not show your real self really is ... weird."

Cali frowned. "Those stories aren't completely made up. Well, I'm not dumb. I just take a little longer to learn, and I would talk if I had someone to talk to. Nobody wants to talk to me. I think it's because I sometimes hold bugs and don't hurt them. I don't see the problem, though. Do you?"

Inez laughed. "I thought that was fake! No one likes bugs! I see why you have no friends! I guess you DID show who you were ... weird!"

Cali began walking again as if she were a bull and the whole world was red. She still saw no reason why bugs were bad. Was that the true reason she didn't have friends, not from her appearance and not from being a teensy bit behind in math. Was that why she was teased so much? Inez's words echoed in her ears as she walked down the hall: No one likes bugs. No one likes bugs. Well, Cali likes bugs! There was no reason not to, as well. Bugs really do make the world go round!

They finally arrived at the school office, in the front of the building. The secretary told them to wait on the bench by the door. The girls sat as far apart as possible, staring at opposite walls and obviously thinking of their fate. Cali couldn't help biting her nails. They were so short that her actual finger was seen on the top. Once when she was little her mom tried putting tape over them to stop her from biting, but she peeled it off. Another time she put on that nail polish that tasted horrible, but Cali wiped it off before it dried. Every year, "stop biting nails" was her New Year's resolution, but every year it didn't work out. It really made Cali feel good in times of pressure, like this one.

Finally, Mr. T., really Mr. Talbot, stepped out of his door and motioned for the quivering girls to come in.

CHAPTER 17

Mr. T.'s office was just as Cali remembered. It was laid back and modern looking, making it less intimidating. It had a meeting table and pictures of people she didn't know on the wall. Mr. T. had a laptop, a small desk, and a window overlooking the playground. Nothing had changed.

Watching him adjust his glasses and stand up straight, Cali knew she'd get a long talk about what she'd done. That was just what teachers did.

"So girls, what did you do this time?" he asked.

Yep. That long boring talk she always heard about on TV or in books she read. Maybe he'd heard of the same things.

"Um, this is my first time getting in trouble like this, Mr. T. It's my second day here, so there was no last time," Inez said, speaking for herself.

She was good at speaking in front of adults, Cali had noticed, from when she spoke to her mom at her house.

"Ah. I'm sorry. But why, may I ask, have you made this the first time?" he asked calmly, obviously wanting a long chat. "Messed up the bathroom, trash-talked, pushed each other?"

"No, we … er … weren't paying attention to … morning assignments," Inez said.

"Well, SHE was the one who was passing notes and talking. They distracted me," Cali said under her breath, just for Inez to hear.

Mr. T. sadly heard it too. "Cali, you can't be looking at other people. Not paying attention to your teacher makes it YOUR problem. You have to ignore the noises around you and listen to what you're supposed to be listening to."

Cali slumped. It really was their fault. Not her fault. She couldn't focus with them gossiping about her, especially since she didn't even have a problem! Now she'd get in trouble, and next Thursday her father, who came all the way across the ocean, would be mad at her and want to leave!

"Inez, is it true that you were talking and passing notes in class?" Mr. T. patiently asked.

"Um, no, well, sort of. We were talking before the teacher started the assignment. Mandy was the one talking during class and she asked me a question when I was trying to pay attention. I didn't want to talk, so I passed her the answer on the note, but by then, I was in trouble. It was Mandy's fault, but she was paying attention to Mrs. Graham while I wrote the note, so she got away with it," said Inez, obviously nervous.

"Ah, but you answered her. You should do what YOU think is right and pay attention. Though you plead 'not guilty', both of you girls should have some kind of consequence. See me during recess, and I'll have a little job for you."

The girls went back to their class and got their assignments for the day from Mrs. Graham. They even worked during music as another punishment from Mrs. Graham, and with all the hard work, recess came soon. They walked down the hall once more to the principal's office, where Mr. T. held two wooden brooms.

"Girls, it's good you remembered to come! There's still some slush from last night's storm on the parking lot ground. I think a nice punishment for you would be to clear the lot of it. Now get to work. If you don't finish, I'm going to keep you after school."

The girls walked out the front door of the school grumbling. The parking lot was huge, not to mention it had teachers' cars in it! They'd have to sweep under the cars!

"This parking lot is HUMUNGOUS!" moaned Inez. "How will we ever finish it all before recess ends? We'll have to stay after school, and I have piano lessons!"

"How about we quit whining and start? I'll take the left, you take the right," Cali said, and they started sweeping through the snowy, goopy slush.

CHAPTER 18

The girls had been working for about 25 minutes when both of them collided, meaning they had finished each of their sides. That was also the moment when recess ended. It was perfect, other than the fact that they had spent their recess sweeping.

"What happened to you? How bad was it?" Mandy asked Inez when they went back to the classroom. Inez ignored Mandy this time and went straight to work, listening to what Mr. T. had said about doing what you, yourself, think is right.

Cali went home, making a beeline for Bug. She couldn't make eye contact with her mom, since Mr. T. made Inez and her take a slip home for their parents to sign, to notify them that their kids got in trouble and were sent to him. Of course, she barely ever made eye contact with her mother anyway. They weren't very close. Mrs. Still was either too busy with her work on the computer, her chores, or, most often, Caius. Cali didn't know what would be the best time to hand the note to her mom. She was always too busy and so stressed. She didn't want to stress her out even more.

Bug needed new pinecones. Lately, Cali had been giving it pinecones from a pine tree down the street. It had plenty, WAY more than her dying pine tree, so she hoped whoever owned it wasn't angry that she was taking just a few for her western conifer seed beetle.

Bug seemed to be doing well. Every day, it was in a new spot in the box, so Cali started putting objects in the box for it to climb on like more pencils, twigs, rocks, and one toilet paper tube that it especially liked. Cali sometimes thought it ran away, but it was just lounging in the tube! Bug was the one that brightened each and every day. It truly made her smile with its curiosity and sheer innocence. Bug filled her loneliness, which was a giant gaping hole in her life.

Just as she had placed Bug's jewelry box back on her dresser and took out her laptop to do her homework, an essay on Native Americans, she heard a knocking on her door. The knocking came from the bottom half of the door, obviously meaning it was Caius. What was he doing knocking at her door when he was banned from her room?

Cali opened the door anyway, and sure enough, there was Caius, holding a macaroni necklace, the ideal craft made in first grade.

"I'm sorry about what happened to your bug. It was cute. I made this for you to make you happier," Caius said in his cute voice he always used with their mom.

Why was Caius being so nice to her all of a sudden? They hated each other! They were mortal enemies! Caius was just born to make Cali's life worse! She couldn't accept this from him!

She did, though, and gave a quick "thank you", with no real pleasure in her voice, like when it's your birthday and your friend gets you the exact opposite of what you wanted and clearly didn't put any thought into the gift, but you didn't want them to feel bad.

That was just weird. He must have some trick up his sleeve! Cali put that out of her mind and set to work on her essay, which was due Friday, but something else was taking up her brain ... the slip had to be signed tomorrow. Cali couldn't forge her mom's signature! That was illegal, but she didn't want her mother to have even more to think about if she found out. Cali didn't want to get in even more trouble that wasn't primarily her fault, so she decided to get her mom to sign the slip.

Mrs. Still was busy making dinner while trying to spend time with Caius at the same time. She really was a miracle woman and could do pretty well without her husband around.

Cali could barely find a voice left in her throat, and she thought her tongue had broken off, but she managed to get her mom's attention.

"C-can you sign th-this, Mom?" she asked, her hand shaking as she gave the form to her mother. Cali could only wait for the screaming reaction and deep sigh of sadness from her mom.

CHAPTER 19

Silence. No screams could be heard. As her mother read over the form, her expression looked as if she were playing poker — and was good at it, too! What was wrong? Could she be holding in an explosion?

Suddenly, a tear rolled down Mrs. Still's left cheek. Then a drop of salty water fell on the right. Cali looked as if she was about to cry, too! Her mom was so disappointed in her that she was crying! Imagine that! This was why Cali didn't want to give the form to her! Oh, why did she? She was a horrible daughter! Now her mother would be more stressed than ever, and right when she should be happy because her husband was coming home soon!

"Oh, Cali," she began.

Cali knew how this would end: "How could you?"

But no, Mrs. Still instead cried "How could I?"

"What?" Cali asked in disbelief. "This is my fault, Mom. I was the one ... not paying attention."

"No, it's my fault for not helping you. I knew you'd lose control someday. Since day one, I knew something was wrong with you. Ever since you lost your little friend, Yasmin, you had no friends! I didn't know why! I thought you were a good kid, but there was nothing I could do. I adjusted my interest to Caius so I could help him be social and have a good life. I just didn't know what to do with you, so I've been avoiding you all these years! I'm so sorry, Cali! I'm so so sorry."

Cali felt like she was going to faint. All of that made her feel lightheaded. Her own mother saw something wrong with her. It really wasn't Cali that couldn't make friends! It was everyone else for not accepting her liking of insects! It wasn't her fault and this had nothing to do with school — she was just distracted!

"Mom, my lack of friends doesn't have anything to do with this! Somebody sitting next to me was just passing notes, which distracted me, so I couldn't pay attention to Mrs. Graham. It isn't about my problems, because I don't have any. Everyone else does!" Cali explained, annoyance in her voice.

Mrs. Still sighed. "Honey, I know you're just denying that you have problems. You can tell your mother, I won't bite. Does it have to do anything with those bugs you used to bring into the house? Don't you know most people aren't such big fans of creepy crawlies?"

Cali felt like erupting. She was ready to blow. Her emotions couldn't be held in a second longer! Bugs are NOT creepy, whatsoever!

"I DON'T GET IT!" yelled Cali, making Caius run out of the kitchen.

Earlier, he had been listening intently to the conversation, but now, Cali saw it was too much for him. Mostly too much for her, though.

"You don't get what, dear?" Cali's mother asked, a quiver in her voice.

Cali had definitely stressed her mom out now, but she didn't care one bit because she was too stressed herself.

Before Mrs. Still got an answer, Cali had already run to her room and plopped on her bed. Her pillow soon became damp with thick tears streaming from her eyes.

Even her mom hated bugs! Everyone did! So why did she find them so interesting, so intriguing, so amazing? What was wrong with her? Why did she have to be so different? She felt like a criminal, an outcast from society!

"Dear, can I come in?" Mrs. Still asked with fear.

Cali knew her mother wanted to help, but this was the first time in her life that she did. She had never been there for her, in fact, nobody had. Her father had left for Afghanistan. Her best friend had left for Iran. The only one that stayed to comfort her was Bug. An insect, an invertebrate, a, if you will, "creepy crawly". The only kind one was a bug. Imagine that.

CHAPTER 20

"No!" sobbed Cali, answering her mother's request to enter her bedroom. She didn't want her mother in her room, not after Cali found out that she, too, was a hater of insects, a person who didn't understand her.

Cali stopped crying to wait for the faint sound of footsteps to leave her door. There was no such sound.

"Why? I can help, Cali! What did I do?" Mrs. Still asked.

"No you can't!" Cali yelled back, but it came out muffled because she was talking into her pillow.

She listened again and this time heard a sigh followed by those much-needed footsteps. They enabled her to look at her "jewelry". She stared as it clumsily hobbled along the box. She gazed so intently that she didn't even notice when her mom called her in for dinner later. Or maybe she just didn't want to notice — you can't be sure.

Bug looked up at her with those small, beady eyes as it crawled up a pencil, slowly, since it was late afternoon. Those eyes weren't big, adorable puppy dog eyes, or narrow, mysterious cat eyes. They were tiny and innocent, but they pierced Cali's heart, and from then on, she knew that she had to let it be known to everyone that insects are amazing little creatures. She just didn't know how.

Cali spent the week trying to avoid people as much as possible. She never talked to anyone, and when someone said "Good morning" to her, she just gave them a little flick of her hand. There wasn't much difference with that from an unwelcoming greeting or shooing someone you don't like away.

On Thursday, Inez left for some other state because she had no friends at Castle Road Elementary. Nobody thought much about it, but Cali gave a little smirk at the thought that *she* had friend problems compared to Inez.

The rest of the week was quite ordinary, since Cali barely talked to anyone anyway, but now she tried not to even look at them. She didn't want to make eye contact with people who discriminated against bugs.

Finally Wednesday came, the day before Mr. Still would finally come home after two years of deployment in Afghanistan. He missed coming home for his birthday last year because the enemy was multiplying, and they needed their best soldiers to fight.

Cali actually didn't see her dad since he left when she was five, since the other years when he came back he just gave his children a quick hug at night before he went on vacation with her mom. This year, though, he'd be staying home, and Cali just couldn't wait! For the most part, at least.

She hadn't seen him in so long and wondered what he'd think of her. He must've heard she had no friends. Would he be disappointed? She truly hoped not! Cali just couldn't wait for his sofa to be filled once more and to hear soothing sounds of him watching football when she fell asleep at night.

While she was straightening up his den so he'd feel at home when he came back, Caius ran over to her. Cali really didn't want to talk to him at that moment, or any moment soon for that matter.

"What does Daddy look like?" he asked quietly.

Cali frowned, but then smiled, thinking to herself.

"What does Daddy look like?" she repeated Caius's question.

"Yes," Caius answered her impatiently. "That's what I want to know. What does he look like?"

Cali wanted to be alone. She didn't want to talk to anyone still. She couldn't get over what people thought of her. And what kind of question was he asking? Then Cali remembered that Caius had only seen short glimpses of their father in blurry pictures, since he left before Caius was born.

"Hmm. Well, to start off, his legs and arms have muscles all over them — huge ones. I'd say they're about the size of a grapefruit each."

"Oh, wow!" exclaimed Caius.

"And his skin is really dark and smooth, since when he's at war, he's in the sun all day."

"Ooh!" cooed Caius. "But what does his face look like?"

Cali paused. "His face? His chin up to his ear is covered in scratchy stubble that feels like you're getting a massage when he kisses you on the cheek. And his eyes are bright blue like the cleanest ocean ... almost like the Caribbean when you can see your toes with the water up to your neck. His eyebrows are thick and light blond, and they match his minimal amount of hair. I don't know why, but he has to shave it to do his job."

Caius looked completely mesmerized. "He sounds awesome!"

Cali nodded. "He is awesome," she said, and went back to dusting, not being able to wait until after school the next day.

Bug

CHAPTER 21

When Cali came home from another quiet yet straining day of school, she was attacked with a big, warm bear hug, and she at once knew who it was. Her mother had picked her father up at the airport while Cali was at school, so he was here now!

"Oh, Cali," he murmured, running his fingers through her hair, but he quickly pulled them out since it was all knotted. "Uh, sorry about that."

Cali giggled. Her father always made her laugh, and it seemed like he hadn't made her laugh in centuries. He hadn't even *been* there in centuries! She gazed up into his clear blue eyes, smiling. Then, Caius came running and screaming in.

"And this is my robot I drew!" he yelled excitedly, waving a scribble on piece of paper in Mr. Still's face.

"I see you've already met Caius," Cali joked.

"Yes, he's a lot different from when he's sleeping! But you and I have a lot of catching up to do!"

Cali frowned. She didn't know if she wanted to talk about her horrible life with her dad. She wanted to make him happy, which would make her happy. She wanted to spend quality time with him one way or another, though. She wanted to make up for all of those years!

They walked to his den and sat on his couch. Caius and Mrs. Still followed, not wanting to miss time with Mr. Still either.

"I don't know where to start, but Mommy told me both of you have been doing great in school and have lots of friends! I'm so proud of you kids!" Mr. Still complimented.

"Oh yeah! I get 100s on all my reading worksheets and my friends are Billy, Tomas, Herby ..."

While Caius bragged, Cali stared at her mom worriedly. She didn't have any friends and was just an average student!

" ... Francis, Phillip,"

"Cali, tell me about you," Mr. Still broke in.

Cali's face turned pale. She couldn't lie. What would she do? She stared at her mother again, who was sweating as well. Cali ran up to her.

"Why did you lie to him?" Cali whispered angrily to her mother.

"I didn't want him feeling worried about his kids while he was serving so he'd do his best! He's a lieutenant you know! He has a lot to think about and doesn't need you on his mind. I'm sorry again. It was for his sake," she whispered back.

"What's going on?" Mr. Still asked impatiently.

"Oh, well, Cali has s-so m-much to tell that sh-she's wondering what to say," Mrs. Still broke in.

"So you still think I have problems? Think I would ruin Dad's work methods with my giant problems? Well I DON'T have problems, so you have NO reason for lying to him! NONE!" Cali whispered loudly, losing her temper again.

She hated being so emotional all the time, especially in a happy time like this, but she couldn't help it. Everyone was so clueless about her and mean!

"I'm no expert, but by the looks of it, you and Cali aren't sorting out what you want to say," Mr. Still said to his wife, who now was blushing massively for many reasons at the moment.

Cali was still fuming. She couldn't control herself.

"Dad, you'd be on my side, right? You wouldn't turn against me like everyone else did? I know you'd think I'm not crazy, right?" Cali demanded of her father.

"It really seems like I've missed a lot. Cal Cal, you were never this angry! What's happened to you? I am on your side! Tell me your problems!" Mr. Still reassured his daughter.

Cal Cal was the name he always used to call her, and she loved it, so she knew he meant business. Mr. Still shooed away his wife and son, so they could have a father-daughter talk.

They settled next to each other on the couch, already making Cali feel better.

"So, what's wrong Cali? You have friends, right? I've heard about them."

Cali sniffed, holding in tears. "Mom was lying. I don't have any friends."

"And why would that be? You're such an amazing and lovable little girl!"

Cali wondered if her dad would understand her problem. "People don't like me because I like bugs. I mean, I don't have them crawling all over me or something like that. That would be weird! I just don't squash one if I see it on the ground. Do you think that's a problem?"

Mr. Still laughed. "Bugs are to be squashed just like the people of Afghanistan! Do you understand, Cali? They're lower than us, evil. They don't deserve to live!"

"But, Dad. Some bugs may seem annoying at times, ones that sting or bite, but some are innocent just like some, and probably most of the people in Afghanistan. Most deserve to live. Most are kind if you look deeper inside them!" Cali explained to him.

"Phooey, I don't know about that!" said Mr. Still.

CHAPTER 22

Cali sighed. She thought her father would understand!

"But dad, don't you see? The whole war, killing so many innocent Afghan and American people, started because of a few really mean ones. And not only soldiers were killed, but bystanders, too. It's not like all of Afghanistan planned 9/11! Just a few mean people did all the damage by themselves, and they were tracked and killed, so it's no more use fighting! It's as if you're walking outside and an evil ant comes up and bites you, (which doesn't really happen by the way). You don't just go and squash its whole anthill! The hill has perfectly decent ants in it!"

Mr. Still thought about that. "Well, what makes you so sure the other ants won't bite?"

"What makes you think they will?" asked Cali confidently.

"Huh. I guess you're right. What have bugs ever done to me anyway?"

Cali smiled her broadest smile since Bug crawled on her. She wrapped her arms around her dad's neck, hugging him gently and resting her head on his muscular chest. "You're so awesome! I never want you to leave!"

They spent the rest of the night, after a delicious family dinner, playing board games. Cali even thought about showing her dad Bug, but she decided it was best not to push it. He said bugs were okay, but he never said they were okay in the house. Plus, if her mom heard, she would surely scream.

While she watched TV with her dad, Cali fell into a deep, calm sleep, as if she hadn't slept in years. He carried her to her room easily and placed her on her bed. She smiled in her dreams. Mr. Still didn't even think twice about the "jewelry box" on her dresser as he went back to his den to watch football until late at night.

The next day, Cali woke up and got ready for an absolutely fun and fabulous day with her dad again. She hadn't forgotten about tending to her other love, Bug, so before anyone else was up, she refilled its sponge and took it out to play. Its cuteness was irresistible, and she couldn't go a day without staring at it.

She ran to the breakfast table after getting dressed and was ready to have a hearty meal with her whole family. But someone was missing ... her father.

"Where's Dad?" Cali asked her mom, who was pouring glasses of milk. Though she didn't want to talk to her mother, she needed to ask this important question. It was also strange that Caius was eating his breakfast so unenthusiastically when he was normally so perky in the morning, which Cali could never understand.

"His best friend got injured on the field. Last night, Daddy rushed on a plane to go see him. He probably won't be back for his birthday ... or at all this year," Mrs. Still said, sighing sadly.

Cali's mouth fell straight to the ground and her legs felt limp like two wiggly (and giant) pieces of licorice. He was finally back ... and gone again! How could he? Right when she recruited another person to her side, they left. It seemed as though no one really did like her — except Bug of course.

Cali didn't have the strength to eat anymore. Her hunger had gone away. She was about to run, crying, to her room, but Caius ran up to her and hugged her gently.

She gasped at his odd behavior. Caius never cared about her, and she, in return, never cared about that chubby, spoiled, attention — getting brat.

"I know how you feel. He *is* my Daddy, too!" Caius said.

Cali looked astonished. She didn't think Caius had it as hard as she did. He *did* have the same amazing dad, so he must feel just as bad that he left. That really was what siblings were for. Yes, to annoy each other sometimes, or most of the time, but they were there to comfort one another and go through hard times together. Maybe Caius even felt bad about Bug's fake death, too!

"C'mon. Let's go to school and forget about all this, like Dad didn't even come yesterday, okay?" Cali told Caius, to reassure him in return for his kindness, but as she brushed her teeth, she didn't know if forgetting it all would be that easy. Being with her dad felt so good, but knowing he understood her appreciation of insects felt even better.

CHAPTER 23

On the bus, Cali still hadn't forgotten. How could she? How could her Dad's friend get hurt at a time like this? It was very inconsiderate! Cali soon realized *she* was being inconsiderate herself. She was getting a bit carried away.

Though carried away, she still had reasons to be angry with everyone for not realizing she was completely sane. Cali avoided everyone on the bus and in her classroom.

During morning assignments, after their daily math assignment, Mrs. Graham announced she was excited about something fun they would be doing. Everyone groaned. A teacher's idea of fun usually was never fun, nowhere near fun to be more specific.

"Everyone will write an oral report to read in front of the class on Monday. You'll have tonight and the weekend to work on it!"

The class sounded as if they were being tortured as their assignment was given.

"But wait! The topic will be something you feel strongly about! I'm sure you'll all like to inform each other about what you enjoy. It'll be quite fun! You may begin your day's work," Mrs. Graham said and walked to her desk to do her mysterious work.

The class seemed to agree that it would be fun. They went into a buzz of ideas for the report. The kids scrambled around to their friends' desks, listening to what everyone would write about. Cali heard a lot of dancing, acting, tennis, and even one person who wanted to write about anime. It was quite a scene, with the gossip of everyone's essay topic spreading to every kid easily like creamy butter on toast.

Cali stayed in her seat and tried to concentrate on math. She hated loud commotion and didn't need to know what other people were doing. She'd hear their report on Monday, and since they were so mean to her, she didn't really care what they were writing about anyway.

All Cali cared about was what she was writing about, which she immediately knew.

She'd write about insects, of course. If she supported her facts well enough about why they were great, she'd definitely convince everyone she wasn't crazy! The one problem was that nobody seemed to care about how many facts she had, how many ants she claimed were cute. They had it super-glued into their brain that bugs = bad. She *had* to write her best and hope to pry (gently, of course) the glued opinion out of their mind.

Cali even overheard some girls talking about what she might write about. That was Linda and Karina.

"Maybe Cali's writing about how she loves being a loser!" Linda guessed, snorting.

"No, that would be good, but she wouldn't admit she's a loser, although *we* all know. I think she might write about her stupid obsession with bugs. Haha! That would be hilarious!" Karina snorted.

How did Karina know? And why would that be funny? It's not! And it's not stupid. It's not an obsession, either! Cali burned with anger again.

Finally, the two bullies walked over to Cali.

"What are you writing about, Cali?" Karina asked, trying to keep a straight face, but she laughed anyway.

"You'll see on Monday," Cali replied quietly, keeping her eyes on her math book.

Linda and Karina walked away laughing.

"Maybe I should bring earplugs for Monday!" Linda commented.

"Just for Cali's report, though!" Karina giggled.

Cali needed them to hear. She needed them to listen and learn and change. She'd make her essay so spectacular and moving that when they see on Monday, their eyes would pop out of their sockets!

Now Cali just had to find a way to make it happen.

CHAPTER 24

Once Cali got home from school, she got to work on the essay. It was actually very easy. There were so many topics she wanted to cover that she never got writer's block, and since her essay came from deep in her heart, she always found the perfect words to use.

She'd finished the essay before she went to bed, not even needing the weekend to work on it. It came easily, and she was proud of it. At night, while she was trying to fall asleep, she said the words over and over in her mind. They seemed convincing. They went together smoothly and made Cali feel proud to have written it. But as she rolled over on her side, she realized they were just words. Would words convince her classmates enough?

She thought about it for a while and decided they'd really have to see that bugs were cute, too, and not just amazing to like them. And it was obvious who the cutest insect was — Bug. If she brought it in, everyone would surely swoon! It was her best bet. She fell asleep feeling confident about her essay and the future, where insects might be loved more.

Monday came fast. Cali was going to be the tenth person to read her report in their class of sixteen, by a number pulled out of a hat. That gave her time to look over her essay, but it also gave time for her to be nervous. Her stomach flipped in circles, her breakfast taking new forms. Cali patted her "jewelry box", which was on her desk. Everyone had shot a funny look at it when she walked in.

The oral essays started right when everyone had arrived, and each was about two minutes. They were nothing special. Elaboration was minimal, and the whole essay seemed made to be yawned at.

Mandy wrote about her cat, Karina wrote about ice — skating, Juanita wrote about gymnastics, Lindsay went on and on about dogs (duh), and they didn't seem nervous at all. Each essay made Cali more nervous. Nervousness tingled and made her feel sick. But she couldn't bail out. Not after she could potentially change the thoughts her peers think of insects forever.

"Thank you, Tim, for your wonderful essay on baseball," Mrs. Graham said, starting the applause as

Tim walked back to his seat from the front of the room.

His was the fifth essay on baseball she'd heard so far, and it sickened her.

"Now it's Cali's turn to read her oral report!" Mrs. Graham announced.

That sickened her even more.

Cali held Bug in its box in one hand, her two-page essay in the other. She walked as slowly as she could to the front of the room. The floor felt like sticky tape, and each step she took, she had to pry her foot off the ground with great force. By the time she got to the front of the room, it felt like she'd already lost loads of energy.

"And what is your essay about, Cali?" Mrs. Graham asked patiently.

"It's about bugs and why I think people should like them," Cali answered, trembling vigorously from head to toe. She didn't like standing in front of audiences whatsoever.

The whole class immediately broke into a sea of laughter. Mean remarks were being passed around about her. Karina even fell over backwards in her seat, after telling Linda she was right and laughing about it.

Cali just had to stand there through it. She didn't want to start reading. At that moment, it seemed like she'd never be able to convince the class anyway, especially since they thought she was a complete dork. They thought it was funny that she was writing about bugs. It made the tears want to start flowing again. Why?

"Class, please settle down and listen to Cali's report. She listened when the rest of you who presented read their reports. Show her your respect and pay attention, please," Mrs. Graham broke in.

The class fell silent, but smirks were still seen, and some were passing notes. This was her cue. She opened her mouth to read ...

CHAPTER 25

"Bugs, as we all know, are everywhere. In the grass, in the sky, in trees, on our bodies, (Yes, things like mites live in our eyebrows), and even in our own homes. Bugs are everywhere you look, even if you don't see them, because some can be microscopic."

The class shuddered. Some covered their ears to block out the rest of the report. Cali just sighed and went on.

"But with so many bugs in this world, no one knows quite how many because around 7,000 new species are found each year, we never stop to think about what they do to help our lives and how they make our days brighter. Most people only think how they make them more annoying, and their reasons don't have good facts to back them up. Then, they kill whatever insect they just saw. It sickens me to see those magical creatures, which take part in our daily lives, squashed for no reason at all, except doing what they're supposed to do, just like we're supposed to go to school. Does anyone feel the same way I do?"

Nobody raised their hand. Juanita stuck out her tongue and laughed quietly, whispering something to Karina. It was probably something like, "why would I think that?" Well, Cali had the answer.

"The truth is, you can't live without insects. And not just because they're everywhere, but because they make our lives much better! For example, you wouldn't have most of the food you eat without insects."

"You mean we eat bugs?!" cried Johnny, who quickly covered his mouth after blurting out his question.

"No, but the fruits and vegetables we eat to stay healthy wouldn't be there without bugs. Insects like bees and butterflies, even some beetles and other bugs pollinate our crops and flowers to make the foods we all enjoy."

"Yes, but bees sting!" commented Linda.

"They only sting if you bother them or go near their hive first. If you're stung, it's your fault for getting in their way!"

Linda frowned.

"Also, without insects, other animals wouldn't have food. They're part of the food chain, so without them, larger animals would die out, too. Nature wouldn't be the same! But besides helping with food, insects help us know when to fix things around the house."

Mandy raised her eyebrows skeptically. "I have ants all around my house. You're saying that's good? You're so weird."

Cali jumped in. "It *is* good, Mandy. If lots of ants or any other swarm of bugs are getting into your house, you probably have insulation problems. If a steady stream of bugs are coming in, that'll show you there's a hole in your house. You could be wasting lots of energy when you turn on the heat in the winter or air conditioning in the summer. It could also show signs of rotting wood in the house's structure, a major problem you discovered you had because of bugs coming in. If you fill up the hole with caulk, by finding where your trail of ants starts, you could save a lot of energy and money! Don't kill the ants in your house, either. Let them go outside where they belong for helping you, and you can even follow where they go in your house. They might lead you to lots of crumbs which could get moldy and really gross."

"Well, what about the bugs outside of your house? Huh? What about them? I have lots of mosquitoes, and I'm bitten all the time! Will I get malaria?!" called out Linda, annoyed, and hoping to stump Cali.

"Those are good, too! Mosquitoes may bite, but they tell you that your lawn is soggy, since the larvae grow up in little pools of water. That can be bad for your grass, so look into getting something to drain the pools of water. If you want to get rid of the adult mosquitoes, buy some dragonfly larvae. Dragonflies will be a pretty addition to your yard and get rid of your mosquitoes in a humane way. For the rest of the insects around your house, that's where they live, and their families were at your property long before you were, so it's their home too, making no reason to harm them."

Cali grinned a small grin. She might just be getting a little closer to convincing them!

"Now, how many people here garden?" Cali asked, and about two hands went up.

"How many people's parents garden?" Cali asked. Seven hands shot up.

"So, gardening is obviously a part of some of our lives, and plants are a part of all of our lives. Trees give us oxygen, shade, and wood for many of the objects we use every day. Trees and plants give us fruits. Plants give us vegetables. Flowers give color to our yards. Worms make the soil clean so we can have all of those plants that we love and need to survive."

"But worms are gross and slimy!" whined Karina.

"Yes, but would you like the world to be full of dead plants, making dead animals that eat plants, and dead animals that eat those animals? No! Worms dig tunnels in the dirt letting in air, water, and nutrients for plants. They also decompose plant and animal matter in the soil that plants can't directly eat so they can eat it and become much healthier. Worms make the plants grow! So, the next time you see one pushed up from the rain, squiggling on the ground, pick it up and put it in the dirt!"

Johnny looked impressed. Someone was catching on! Yes! Cali thought the next part of her report would really show some people!

"So, now you see how insects help us. Some of you may still think they're still gross and dumb and mean."

Most of the class nodded or said "yes I do".

"Insects are not dumb. Some are actually very intelligent, take honeybees. They have a very good memory and a language to help them pass on the locations of fields with flowers. Monarch butterflies must be smart to know where to go on their huge migration to the south and north each year and how to survive in many places. Praying mantises need lots of intelligence to stalk and hunt prey. And although many disagree, the American cockroach is brilliant and has many stealthy survival skills. I also think spiders must be smart (although they aren't insects, people call them bugs, though) to make those gorgeous, intricate webs, and just to maneuver with all of those legs. That goes for millipedes and centipedes, too!"

"Yeah, so what if some bugs have an itty bitty brain that functions nowhere near as well as a human brain does? Bugs still aren't smart enough to be kind creatures that do good deeds for one another or help each other out! They aren't smart enough to be nice and lend a helping hand, or even socialize at all! That makes them dumb and mean!" protested Juanita matter-of -factly.

Cali just went on talking to prove Juanita and the others wrong once again.

"Some insects are very social, even eusocial, the highest form of sociality in the animal kingdom. In fact, besides insects, there are only two types of eusocial animals: the naked mole rat and the Damaraland mole rat! In insects, there are bees, ants, wasps, termites, and weevils that are all highly cooperative and kind to each other."

"Yeah, but bugs are still gross! I hate them!" yelled Mandy.

"Well, have you ever looked at them really closely? Have you ever seen their adorable black eyes? Have you ever felt the constant thumping of their antennae? If you did, I assure you that you'd think bugs were cute!" Cali answered.

Mandy didn't look convinced. "Well, where will I find a bug to do that?" she asked, laughing at her own question. She obviously didn't want to try.

Cali answered anyway. "Right here! I brought an insect that I've been taking care of in my room for a long time now. It's a western conifer seed bug, and its name is Bug! It's the cutest and most amazing insect I've ever seen!"

Cali took Bug out of the box, waiting for her response.

CHAPTER 26

"Aieee!" shrieked Karina. "Put it back! Put it back! Kill it! Kill it!"

Cali wanted to lay down and die. She'd finished her report, took out Bug, and still no one understood her. Was it really that she was just different? Was it that nobody would ever understand her? There was something wrong with her. She'd have to be rushed to the hospital right away. She'd been living too long with the love of bugs. She needed liposuction to get it pumped out of her. It should pump out her loneliness from all of her years. Then maybe the hole would fill back up with a better life. A normal, happy life surrounded by friends, family, and fun seemed so far away.

She followed Karina's first command and opened Bug's box back up to put it in. Bug wouldn't get off her finger. Suddenly her eyes met its. Cali's world froze as she gazed into the shiny beads upon

Bug's slender head. They looked cute to her. They made her happy. They helped her feel important. Bug had shown her innocence. It had been the only one there for her for weeks. It had made her laugh when all she wanted to do was cry.

Cali snapped back into reality. Only a few seconds had gone by. They were amazing seconds. She wanted to go back in time and relive them.

She felt like a deer in the headlights in the front of the room. She felt misplaced and unwanted — like an insect.

But suddenly, Whitney yelled from her place in the back of the room: "Karina, that's mean! Bug is cute! Now I don't think bugs are gross any more. They're actually pretty cool! Just be quiet, Karina!"

Cali was astonished. Somebody actually cared! She'd changed someone! She'd done it! There was another person on planet earth that really understood her perfectly! Cali felt like she was floating on a cloud! She was swimming in sunshine and happiness and pleasure! The feeling was like no other!

Martin jumped in. "You're right! Karina, didn't you hear how awesome bugs are from Cali? Didn't you listen to what she was saying? If you did, you'd see how bugs are super little dudes!"

Suddenly, everyone started adding their own view as to why Karina was wrong. Cali couldn't believe her ears. She pinched herself numerous times, but it was no dream. She had truly convinced everyone that bugs were great! Maybe it actually was a dream ... her dream come true!

Karina soon was crimson. She hid her face under her own oral report. Only her short, light brown pigtail could be seen. Cali smiled. She wanted to laugh. She wanted to dance. Everything had turned out perfectly!

"Class, please settle down. Thank you, Cali, for that very informative oral report on insects. You've taught us all a lot! You may go back to your seat. Whitney, it's your turn," Mrs. Graham announced.

Cali put Bug back in the box before she walked to her seat. As she strolled across the room, everyone wanted to see Bug. They cooed when they did. Cali couldn't stop beaming. Her mouth was sore from her wide grin.

The walk back to her seat felt so much faster than her walk to the front of the room, even though she stopped at almost everyone's desk along the way. How great she felt. She felt like she'd conquered the world. She wasn't weird. She was a decent person!

As Whitney read her oral report, Cali opened Bug's box once more. Bug was on its sponge, looking quite content.

"I did it," Cali whispered to her tiny friend. "Wait, sorry. We did it!"

Bug thumped its tiny antennae on the sponge.

Bug

EPILOGUE

Cali's life had only gone uphill from the day she read her oral report. People talked to her more. Nobody thought of her as strange or different. She felt equal.

It seemed like the kids had really listened to the essay. Cali even saw Mandy pick a worm up off the street one rainy day and put it on the grass. Of all people, Mandy? It made Cali even happier.

And yes, it was rain! Though it was only February, the days had gotten much warmer. There wasn't an inch of snow to be seen! Most people didn't even need to wear their thick winter clothes any more. It was crazy!

On February 25th, Cali decided that it had been warm for a very long time, and it probably wouldn't be cold again. Animals had started coming out, and that showed it was time. It was time to let Bug go. It could find pinecones on its own now and live in the wild. Though Cali loved Bug immensely, she had to let it go for its own good. She knew it was the right thing to do.

At night, after dinner, she asked her mom if she could go outside and look at the moon for a project for school. She truly *was* studying the moon in school, but her real reason to go out was to release Bug.

Once her mom allowed Cali to go outside alone for just ten minutes primarily to study the moon's current phase, she darted out the door with her "jewelry box" held tightly in her hands.

She set the box down on the ground when she came to the dying pine tree in her yard. She would have released Bug in the giant conifer down the street, but she wanted it to be closer to her.

The moon was directly above the tree. It was a waxing gibbous, shining a large reflected pool of light over Cali.

Cali opened Bug's box. Bug was scurrying around like crazy, climbing confidently on everything in the box. This was why Cali chose this time of day. It was Bug's time.

Cali placed her hand in the box. Bug crawled right onto her finger. Its fast movements tickled hugely. Cali couldn't seem to laugh, though. She was all choked up.

"Bug, I have to release you now. It's warm out. You can roam free. You'll love it outside. It's better than a little box."

Bug started up Cali's arm.

"You've helped me so much. I've changed because of you. I am because of you!"

Bug made its way to Cali's shoulder.

"I love you, and I'll never kill an insect — ever. Bugs are the greatest creatures on earth. And whoever doesn't agree, well, you know that if they see you, they will."

Bug now had crawled down Cali's arm, almost at her hand.

"So, go now. Find yourself a nice, juicy pinecone."

Cali let Bug onto the grass near the conifer. Bug didn't move, though. It stood still in the whispering breeze. Cali stood still as well, watching carefully.

"Cali, come in now! I'm sure you've identified the moon by now!" Cali heard from inside the house.

She took a glimpse of Bug, who was still standing in the grass.

Cali wanted to run over and scoop Bug up, hold it one more time. Bug was her happiness and her true passion. How could she just let it go?

Cali wondered if Bug didn't even want to be outside. What if it wanted to be with her, too! She could still keep it in her room. She'd fetch it pinecones and fill its sponge. She'd take it out every day, and talk to it, and give it objects to climb on and play with! Would that be better?

Before Bug was completely out of sight, Cali looked at it one more time, hoping it had followed her, or even had stayed in the same spot, sad that Cali had left it.

But Bug had started up the pine tree's trunk, antennae happily fluttering.

A tear rolled down Cali's cheek, the faintest of smiles on her face. She headed inside.

The End

THE STORY OF TWIDDLE MY WESTERN CONIFER SEED BUG

Why did I choose to write about western conifer seed bugs, of all insects? And why bugs?

What gave me the idea for the portions of the book having to do with insects came from my own intense love of bugs. Ever since I was in preschool, I always liked looking for bugs, holding them, naming them, looking up what species they are, and playing with them. My friends always thought I was super weird, so I was made fun of sometimes and definitely humiliated! The ant scene was actually completely true! I shudder as I think about it!

But I hadn't thought of writing a story about bugs until my western conifer seed bug, Twiddle, died.

I had found Twiddle in my family room in the winter. I couldn't put it in my basement (there are huge black spiders in it), I couldn't leave it upstairs (somebody might accidentally kill it), and I couldn't put it outside (it'd freeze!). I decided to keep Twiddle in a little "Bug Playground" in my room. Just like Cali, I would release Twiddle when it got warm.

The bug playground was a little see — through box that had all different mini playground equipment made just for bugs. It was adorable! I could watch Twiddle from my bed now.

Like Cali, I put a small sponge in the box (which I always saw Twiddle on), and it was very hard for me to find pinecones, since they were so small in the winter months. I didn't replace them much, because it was super hard trudging through the knee — high snow (we had a lot of snow this winter. Plus, I never saw Twiddle eating or any pinecones messed around with. Only once did I see a pinecone with a hole in it. Although, it could have come like that from the pine tree. I hoped it had come from Twiddle.

Bug was completely based on Twiddle's comedic and adorable actions. Pretty much everything Bug did in the story, Twiddle did. I soon learned that western conifer seed bugs were nocturnal. I'd see Twiddle in the same spot all day (maybe it would move its legs once or twice), but the next day, it was in a totally new spot! In the early morning and early evening, Twiddle crawled all around the box on everything! Its clumsy yet persistent way of walking was so cute and made me fall in love with my little bug. My favorite part, though, were the antennae.

Unlike Bug, Twiddle didn't get to be released back into nature. Shortly after a hilarious incident when it got lost and a day later, I found it crawling on my bed, Twiddle died. I sobbed. Twiddle had been such a big light in my life, and I truly wanted to see it released.

I told my friends at school about Twiddle's death, and I got no sympathy. People just made fun of me for keeping a bug in my room.

That sparked my idea to write Bug. I was fed up with people's misunderstanding and hatred of insects. I needed some way to show them that insects are great, with my favorite insect of all — western conifer seed bugs!

I hope you've changed your views on bugs forever!

About the Author ... Hannah Rappaport

Hannah Rappaport lives with her parents and pet hermit crab, Dizzy, in Orange CT. Being the 11 year old she is, she loves hanging out with her friends but also writing (of course), drawing, singing, playing piano and guitar, and acting. Her dad is an author, too, and you can find both his books and Hannah's first book, <u>Are Questions That Bad?</u>, on Owlking.com, or Hannah's own website, GVOAHN.com for vegetarians like her (she immensely loves animals, and could NEVER eat them). Most of all, she will always keep writing because she can tell messages in her stories!